I Never Sold My Soul, but I'll Give You This

Makade Mi'ingin

To My Chief Executive…

1

Aaniin (hello), my name is Makade Mi'ingin, also known as "Black Wolf," a name given to me while I was in prison by a visiting elder. I was born on May 21, 1980, in the United States.

I am addressing you today as a member of your Tribe. To be quite honest, I've always felt like an alien, out of place and out of step, more machine than man. This is my story. What follows is my last and only report of my observations. Over the years, I have been identified, categorized, investigated, poked, and prodded with foreign objects, injected with foreign substances, branded, and placed in state institutions. My journey has carried me through incarceration and into the world beyond, far from the shelter, warmth, and security of our territories.

I have learned to speak English quite well. I have mostly forgotten my own language, but I pray you understand me and receive this in good spirits.

All we, as a people, anywhere, want to be is who we are. So here I am.

Native lives, Black lives, Asian lives, Middle Eastern lives, Caucasian lives, European lives, everyone, everywhere are still held in the balance of the wills of men all around the world, no matter who you are. We're all treated as property in bulk still among the federal and state civil and criminal jurisdictions. Who is entitled to what. Who gave birth to whom. Who stepped into which jurisdiction. Files and cases stacked high, waiting to be solved.

I agree. Solve them.

Resolve them to reach a final accounting. But when that final accounting comes, or when someone is faced with a claim, who really holds the checkbooks? Do the checkbooks even matter in government versus civilian conflict?

Governments look at situations from a global perspective. They have the ability to zoom in with high-powered satellites, capture license plate numbers, record bank robberies in live action, and even simulate realities to create strategies based on proposed narratives.

Yet in their greater quest for good, they often forget something important. They lose sight of the fact that individual people are the reason for their presence in the first place. Individual people are the true balance of power between good and evil.

We must stand against expressions of force to move goodwill forward. We must all recognize that we each of us carries a part of that balance, and that we have to navigate the void together.

According to U.S. treaties with American Indian people, the intent was that Native people would be allowed to live freely. I must report that is not the case once you are identified as American Indian.

I was identified early in my life.

My life has been a constant struggle to exist.

***

My first memory of being investigated by doctors was through the Bureau of Indian Conditions. I was maybe four years old then.

I tested "off the charts," as their people said. Genius-level intellect is what they called it. They told me I could be anything I wanted to be.

At first, I didn't know what I wanted to be. I thought I was already myself, so of course I was confused.

I grew up in the ghettoes of Minneapolis. I was born to a mother who was an alcoholic and to a man who only deposited sperm and left. There was no future care to be had from him, so I was left to find my own way after birth.

My mother's name is Karen. She's currently working her way through life with the person she chose as her soul mate. His name is Tom. To be honest, I never talked with him much. From what I understand, though, he is a U.S. War Veteran, or at least someone who has served. So, if you happen to read this, I definitely salute you, Sir.

[Sidebar:]

It's odd. Veterans acknowledge there is a "School of Hard Knocks," but who serves as the life ambassadors of these people? Who are the living veterans who continue carving out their paths?

***

Karen is still living somewhere in Minneapolis, I believe, or maybe in a suburb. Then again, I'm not doing much better myself these days.

One of my earliest memories is of her running down the alley in my hometown one summer night, holding a bloody knife. I was perhaps four years old.

I looked past her and saw a body lying against a garage in the shadows. She quickly grabbed me and turned me back toward home.

I was never sure what I saw that night, but I shrugged it off. I never understood what happened with that situation afterward. All I know is I was shuffled off to foster care and other institutions soon after. Nobody wanted me in their lives. I was always underfoot, asking questions, trying to figure out what was going on. I got lost in mazes, searching for answers that no one seemed willing to give.

I'd have to say she was an alcoholic like no other. Sometimes I would not see her for weeks, even months. When she did come home, she reeked of booze and yelled at me for not cleaning up this mess or that mess, or for not taking care of my brother. To be honest, I didn't even know I was supposed to. She was never there before, and she never left instructions. More often than not, I got beatings instead.

***

Sure, taking care of my brother felt natural enough, but the funniest story I can recall happened one summer while my mother was out. I decided to cut my brother's hair.

But when I did so, I did it in patches. Scissoring chunks of hair off in randomly spaced intervals. He had had long flowing locks before that.

When I heard my mother coming home, I realized something was wrong with my cutting job. I panicked. I certainly didn't want another beating. I looked around frantically.

In the corner of the medicine cabinet was a jar of some clear gel. I smeared it on my brother's head, pressed the cut hair back into place, and pulled a stocking cap over it. I quickly checked if he looked "okay" and sent him out.

The cover didn't last long. My mom instantly started wondering why he had a stocking cap on in the middle of summer and yanked it off his head.

That night, I got the worst beating ever with an extension cord. My brother had his head shaved down, leaving only a ducktail. The beating I took, by some perspectives, could be considered legendary. She chased me through the house, striking me with the cord until bloody red welts formed everywhere her authority landed.

There we were, running around the small central column that divides the cooking space from the living room and the hallway to the bathroom. I felt like I had to run for my life right in my own home, all because I tried to learn how to cut hair.

I tripped when my sock snagged on a loose screw in the metal trim that separated the cheap linoleum tile from the carpet.

Whap. Whap. Whap.

I felt the strikes instantly. After a few more, I tuned out.

Not long after this event, I was shuffled off to yet another place. I cannot recall which one it was, only that it was in the inner city. I did not last long there. Within days of being sent somewhere new, I would develop the urge to escape. I felt confined, restrained against my will. I had never given my consent for any of this.

Another time, during her absence, I set fire to my own bed by trying to relight a smoke bomb. I had no idea why, but I had to see if there was fuel left in the obviously spent mechanism of chemical elements before me.

The fire department came quickly and put it out. I was left without a bed.

That night, I received one of the worst chasings and beatings yet, this time with a vacuum tube extension. She hit me until it broke.

I remember running in fear as my enraged mother chased me, slapping my backside with the tube. Throbbing red welts formed instantly. I heard the tube crack and splinter against my skull.

Somehow, I remembered the door behind the furnace in her bedroom closet. I could get through it, but she could not. I ran for it, screaming at the top of my lungs, fending off the swings of the tube. I barely made it through when I felt a whoosh by my head. I looked back just in time to see shards of her glass ashtray explode against the doorjamb as I scrambled down the stairs and out the front door. It was about 8:45 pm.

I made it to a payphone several miles away with nothing but bare feet and the stuffed dog that I was lucky enough to be holding onto and had never let go of.

Luckily, a man in a Dusty's Pest Removal truck saw me and took pity. He finished driving me the few blocks it was to my aunt and uncle's house.

I had not even realized it was the first week of November. I can only imagine the sight I made: a tear-stained, dirty little boy, covered in red welts, carrying a stuffed dog, barefoot. I must have looked lost.

Thankfully, the man did not ask many questions. He simply made sure my family was truly my family and left me in their care.

My family let me crash there while my mom cooled off, or drank and did drugs. I never knew which, but it was her thing.

Back home, I never thought it fair to receive her authoritative beatings. I had to sleep on the floor after that since the bed was gone. It took some time before we could replace it. I got used to sleeping on the floor or the couch, wrapped in blankets when the heat was out. What I remember most is bouncing between shelters and the many apartments my mom rented.

My grandfather worked as a janitor at a North Minneapolis Indian Center on Broadway. In his younger days, he was also a boxer and a welder. He would tell me about his fights in the ring.

More often, though, he shared stories of his brother Leonard, who had passed some time before. One story I heard often was how Leonard once strung my grandfather up in a tree. There he was, hanging and struggling to breathe, while Leonard laughed maniacally. It took my great-grandfather several moments to cut him down.

Leonard was later killed in Minneapolis sometime in the early 70s. From what I know of my great-grandfather, he was a bootlegger who made and sold alcohol during the Prohibition Era.

My grandfather would bring home reams of paper to draw on, paints I rarely touched, and pencils I needed to express my visions or communicate what I was trying to say.

We both spoke English very well, but sometimes I would slip into gibberish. That was fine with him. He still took the time to understand me, even though his eyes were tired and he was no doubt exhausted from his day.

Often, I sketched spaceships and other monsters. Sometimes, even technical drawings. Whole worlds grew from the page, quickly evolving.

***

I was often left in the care of my aunts and uncles growing up, or simply left to do my own thing. Other times, I was shuffled to and from shelters. My mother was absent for most of my childhood. I would go weeks, sometimes months, without seeing her. I was left to care for my brother and myself, figuring out how to prepare food with whatever was left behind. I was only about eight at the time.

We lived in a then crappy, run-down brick building in Northeast Minneapolis. It's since been "renovated" by the newer crowds that inhabit the walls.

Once, I became so sick and feverish that I grew delirious. My brother found me in the laundry room on the bottom floor of our three-story building. I was lying in the laundry tub, trying to cool down.

Thankfully, my brother managed to get me all the way upstairs and into bed. He is four years younger than me.

During my confinement to that bed, I experienced the most sensational visions.

At that time, our apartment was across from a large park that had once also been a cemetery. It was a windy night, and I envisioned the trees holding a ceremony, dancing and swinging their branches to the heavens. I envisioned this whole scene being played out, for my benefit, it seemed, right across the street.

The next day, I woke up. The fever had broken, and I was back at play.

Once, when I had not cleaned my room, my mom jabbed me square in the eye with the foot of her crutch. To be fair, my room was a mess, but I never felt she was justified in that.

Over time, she hit me with all sorts of things, whatever was in reach. Extension cords, vacuum tubes, ladles, and even her own hands. I always interpreted that as authority. I never wanted to be an authority myself. The receiving end of authority hurts.

***

My cousins and I would play at the park in their neighborhood, and we spent hours on hide-and-seek inside the house. Basketball in the front driveway with the neighbor kids was always fun. It seemed odd at the time, but many of them gravitated toward me.

In truth, I have always been different.

My aunt, closest in age to me, acted as a sister, a mother, and sometimes a tormentor. Once, while attending the funeral of another aunt who had passed away, she made me ride in the back of the hearse with the coffin. I believe I was only eight at the time. To this day, I still try to scare her whenever I get the chance, just to get her back for that.

"Remember that one time you were on your way to work? Bwahahaha!!"

I had other close friends who have come and gone over the years as well. Myron and Nancy Little, may you forever rest in peace. Their children live on.

At one time, I considered them family, even another home away from home. I called them mom, dad, brothers, and sisters. We often played hide-and-seek in their house. It felt big compared to the tiny apartments my family and I shared.

Over time, our connections have grown distant, but I will always remember those days growing up. I still see your posts on social media. Sometimes I drop a thumb or a comment, but you never return any.

2

I spent a few years in and out of the shelters sponsored by veterans. I never understood why; I was just told I had to go.

I made a friend there early on. Her name was Desiree. I'm sorry, it's been many years, and I've long forgotten her last name, but I knew her spirit very well.

She was African American and also had a troubled past. In her talks with me, she would describe how she was taken from her home and sexually abused. From what I've heard, this is now called human trafficking. She was such a hurt soul, only looking for a place of comfort.

I cherished the times we spent walking in the fields in our immediate vicinity and roaming where we wished, returning to the shelter only when the dinner bell rang.

Desiree had a melanin deficiency that depigmented her skin in splotches. Everyone who looked at her turned away. I'd often see her asking adults for help, only to be quickly shunned away, or worse, not even acknowledged.

Perhaps she just had a quiet voice. In our conversations, she was reserved and soft-spoken, but she would burst into laughter if I made a funny observation.

We often spent time in the pines that bordered the shelter, with the wilderness stretching beyond. Sometimes we played hide-and-seek, other times we just talked about our hopes and dreams. I later discovered she loved writing as much as I did.

As our friendship grew, we created stories among the trees. We imagined maps, charted voyages, and walked paths that seemed to lead everywhere. We acted out our adventures in the pines, collapsing in laughter and joy when we were tired, or running back for food when we heard the dinner bell.

There was also a rope swing. It hung about forty feet up, with a branch cut off about fifteen feet below it. We would climb onto that branch and swing out into nothingness.

One day, I was up in that tree, preparing to swing out. Maybe the person below didn't see me on the branch, but they ran and jumped onto the bottom of the rope. I lost my footing.

I had only a loose hold on the rope. I grasped and fumbled, trying to catch it again.

I fell interminably as I kept grasping for that rope. Trying desperately to gain a grip.

I fell what felt like an eternity, reaching desperately for the rope. At last, I secured my grip, burning the palms of my hands as I slid down the rest of the way.

I do not know how far I had fallen, but when I looked up, everyone was gathered around me. They said I had the wind knocked out of me, that I was gasping for air, that I had been out.

Their faces were shocked when I jumped back to my feet. I honestly had no idea. It didn't seem to faze me.

I looked around, past the wide-eyed stares and open mouths, searching for my one friend. But Desiree was nowhere to be seen.

People later told me that she was the one who grabbed the rope and caused the fall. I searched everywhere for her. I wanted to explain that I was okay, that nothing was wrong.

The staff at the shelter later said she was missing. Some weeks after that, I recall hearing the announcement. Her body had been found on the side of the road. She had been hit by a vehicle, and that was all I was ever told.

After the loss of my one friend, I forever secluded myself in books thereafter. If Desiree taught me anything in knowing her, it was to keep going.

***

While at yet another placement at the hands of the State, I met a couple of friends I still remember to this day. If you happen to read this, Larry, I'm sorry I never made it to Fort Lauderdale when we turned twenty-one. I really did intend to.

Larry was pretty funny, and we were the same age. We would fold our legs with our feet on top of our thighs and walk around on our knees. I usually managed a few steps before falling. My real trick, though, was flipping my eyelids inside out. The looks I got from adults when I popped into their vision that way, the shock and surprise, were always priceless.

I disliked the punishments, though.

Often, I would be forced to write stories while on punishment for my intrusions into adult life. I'd be forced to sit at a table and write.

If I didn't complete a story a day, they only needed to be a paragraph or two, I'd have to sit until I did two the next day, or as many as were due.

Once, I believe I sat on that table for an entire week, refusing to write. I think the intent was to encourage my creativity instead of treating me like a pesky kid. But I often saw it as punishment. It felt like it was killing my creativity, man.

The other kids would walk by as I sat there, drawing at words on the page just to get started. Admittedly, some of that was my own stubbornness. But looking back now, was it really? The authority figures would read my stories. Sometimes they laughed, sometimes they cried, and other times they shrugged them off and put them in my folder behind the desk. I never knew where those stories went after that.

Since I was underage and not at home, I had no choice but to listen. They even opened a special bedroom just for me, with a table all to myself.

Prior to this, I had been in the normal two-bed dorm-style rooms. The new space was no better than a storage cell that had been cleaned out and fitted with a bed. I could not leave that tiny area except to shower or eat.

I tried squiggles, jiggles, jots, dots, free-association, every technique I could think of; most times, I'd just pencil something out, quickly grabbing a character and an arc for which they would travel. Leprechauns would end up in volcanoes, and dragons could burp out gold coins if you hit them in the right spot. Anything I could imagine, just to get off that table.

People create for the love of creating, not because they should have to, right? I grew to dislike writing.

***

I longed to hear the stories of my people. I knew my skin was different in color from most, but I did not know why. I read whatever I could find, wherever I could find it. None of my elders at the time knew the stories either.

In my early childhood, we didn't even know we could be enrolled in a Tribe, let alone that we had cultural histories. Tribal sovereignty in the Urban Area, as it later came to be called, was a null concept. But we, as a family, always banded together. Most of my life, I never saw my mother. I was lost and raised in the system.

Disconnected.

Because our words were spoken more than written, our Native stories had already been washed away from me. By then, I am sure I would not even have recognized them or myself. Some days, I could not even look at myself in the mirror.

At around eleven years old, I adopted the camouflage of those days, which was then called grunge. I was released back into my mother's care, and she had a new apartment. It was our fifth new place in just a few short years.

I started venturing further, and further away from home, eager to explore. Eventually, I would find myself in our urban environment. I was often attracted to the skylines and the people. Often, I would just ride my bike or walk.

The scenery along the paths I chose was often beautiful. I soaked it in as I walked the railroad tracks, wandered down Monroe, or followed any meandering path I could find. I would go anywhere my feet carried me.

The city does have a good trail system, and the guardians of this territory maintain it well. To the guys on the mowers, I have walked past you. I often said hello while snapping a mental picture of something nearby, or nodded at your name tag, quietly saying your name to myself as I captured the moment in memory.

***

Some of the neighbor girls called me dirty because of the color of my skin. It hurt at the time, but I would just smile and crack a joke to ease the tension and move on. I would have felt guilty if I had hurt their feelings in return. Besides, I was attracted to one of them.

Later, we ended up going on a few "dates," as they were called. Our first was to see the movie Benny & Joon at a dinner theater. We had managed to turn a YMCA outreach trip, a group field trip, into a fun evening of movies and burgers.

The movie kind of described this wacky, ideal couple that grew to love each other over the course of their relationship. Later, we also watched The Mighty Ducks.

On school buses, I was often carried from one part of the city to another. Sometimes the route took us along 94 East, other times south on Third Avenue through the city. Looking back, I have no idea why. It always seemed up to the driver's discretion.

From my seat, I saw movies being filmed, buildings going up, foundations being poured, monuments to humanity being planted, and familiar faces replaced with new ones. Dvorak Pharmacy and many other mom-and-pop shops along Central Avenue, north of Broadway to Lowry and beyond, eventually gave way to police stations, large corporations, and bands of individuals who learned to protect each other.

Some people describe this as selling out.

Maybe it's just people recognizing their times as well…

In my neighborhood, three notable movies were filmed: Fargo, The Mighty Ducks, and Lionheart. I watched these movies come together in bits and pieces, created into bigger scenes to be beamed into my eyes through the magic of light and sound.

I am pretty sure some of my educators didn't like me, but I believe they saw my potential even then. Most of them left me alone to play with my crazy ideas. That I was entitled to an American Dream. My American Dream could be manifested, I was told.

Could I somehow be the big guy, the guy that's able to place a sign on his desk that reads: "The buck stops here?"

"Head honcho in charge," President of the U.S.?

Yes, I was told.

I was stunned.

How could one man hold that much power? He must have strong relationships with his neighbors, I pondered. But then I learned that that man's power is limited by people in other branches of the government.

Hold the bacon, what? I reeled. What does that mean?

I read further in the Constitution that people signed; a person may be President if they are a natural born citizen who has reached thirty-five years of age. That's it. Those are the job qualifications. But I must work hard.

Work, I wondered, what is that? I had to learn.

As I write this, I'm forty years of age. COVID-19 is rapidly spreading around the Globe, and some are seriously fearing there's nothing left. Well, there is always hope. I write this in full

acknowledgement of being a person born inherently to walk this Earth. Forever intertwined with those who walked with me.

***

I played with my ideas from then on; I soaked in the wisdom encapsulated in these institutions they call schools. It's a funny thing, schools. They are there, they say, to teach us how to think, not what to think.

I looked at most of the group advertisements and clubs as just advertising to get me involved with that particular aspect. But I never signed up anywhere; I never felt as if any of those activities called to me as a person. Some were downright politically inclined.

In grade school, I mostly attended Hans Christian Andersen Elementary. I was in the "D" program. The "D" was generally reserved for those who didn't belong. In that school, I believe there were four separate letter academies, all segregated.

Deep inside that school is a dungeon. A room exists there filled with cells.

From my recollection, there were four locked cells and four or six "open-faced" cells.

I found myself in these cells a few times, including the locked ones. At that time, it was manned by two guys, one black, the other white. I recall the black guy as being bigger; the white guy seemed average. The black guy was pretty chill, though. He'd tell jokes when the white guy wasn't around in an effort to get us to relax, open up, or chill.

I wish I could recall their names, but it's been so long.

I don't recall being violent at that time, but I would get physically restrained at times, then thrown in one of the cells. I never wanted to stay in school. It was often during my exits that I would be restrained from that liberty.

Once, I "let" them put me in the cell, but quickly escaped.

I had noticed that in putting me in, the white guy left the keys hanging in the lock. Perhaps the other guy had the day off; I cannot recall. But I do not remember him being there that day.

I, of course, didn't want to be either. If adults can take days off, why can't I? I kept kicking and thrashing while being carried.

I didn't hit or kick him, just at the air. He had been carrying me with his arms locked around my torso and under my arms from the back.

He set me down.

I quickly dropped my act, ducked between his legs, scrambled out, and locked him in. I threw the key in the trash by the desk and ran out.

I made my escape. I ran to the end of the hall and kicked the bar on the door, forcing it open, and ran.

As my school was located on the other side of the city, I would use the towers of Downtown Minneapolis to navigate there, and then find my way home. Along the way, I would pass by people of all sorts. Some I would briefly chat with. I relished walking with the people of my city.

My favorite person was the Conga drum player who used to play outside of the Crystal Court on Nicollet Mall. He never shared his name, only his love of rhythm. Passersby would congregate and feel the soul of this musician in his beats. People would sing along or dance, or drop money in his bucket and keep strolling. It truly was a sight to see this man doing what he loved.

***

After the incident of escaping school, when I went back the next day, I was recognized by a school counselor named Sarah as a person who might benefit from helping others more than myself. She asked me if I wouldn't mind assisting people who had disabilities; in return, I would get to spend extra time playing on the video game system she kept in her office. A Nintendo.

I eagerly agreed.

It was exciting because at that time, Nintendo game systems were something quite new, and my family certainly couldn't afford to get one for me.

I quickly found video games enthralling. They were graphic and violent. I much preferred the cartoony violence at first.

Advertising systems often use mascots to make violence seem acceptable to children. Imagine a plumber running around smashing turtles and eating mushrooms. Or a mascot from a favorite pizza chain starring in a video game filled with cartoonish violence, running around, and slapping people with a yo-yo.

It was ludicrous, but it was engaging.

I'd get lost for hours exploring the physical rules of these virtual spaces, trying to find "bugs" or "glitches" that would let me exploit the game's resources. At that time, everything was put out as software encoded on printed circuit boards and sold as is. People still found ways to hack the code or emulate these programs, eventually.

Initially, school was great. I relished in the admiration of creating a work and finding a value in that, in achieving a good grade.

One educator in middle school, Mrs. Hopkins, really kind of let me do my thing; she even recommended me for the Gifted and Talented Education Program.

While attending this program, I was exposed to a lot of ideas that truly gave me the groundwork to navigate among the stars as our people once did. I enjoyed shop classes, physically making things, crafting things from clay, making patterns therein, finishing and polishing these things to fruition, as well as a number of higher-level courses: BASIC Programming Language, Logical Thinking, Math, and Science.

I also played in the Chess Club at school.

I wasn't that good at Chess, but I tried. I think over time I'll get better, so long as I keep working at it.

****

School, for me, was overall a good idea. It was not unlike going to an elder of our Tribe or a family member and asking for advice, as I would later realize. The educators listened to me, tried to figure out what I was asking, and helped me with the problems set before me, either to guide me through the lesson or simply to get me out of their way.

Some of my educators have even said I responded well to challenges. I took that as a testament to my will and spirit; politely said thank you, as I was taught by my elders, and shuffled off on my "Chevro-legs" to learn more.

One time while visiting my reservation "up north," as we called it since I was born in the Twin Cities, I got lost in the backyard of my great-grandmother's house with my brother and cousin.

We ran around in circles for hours, trying to find our way back. Our relatives eventually had to send a search party out to find us.

When they did, it turned out we were only about fifty feet from the entrance to the woods. I remember them shunning us and making jokes at our expense because we had managed to "get lost" in the backyard.

I acted like I didn't understand and kept playing.

Sometimes we still share this story to lighten the mood while playing pool or throwing darts.

***

Back at school, I soon ached for more, to know more. My mind was fed by the world around me; my soul felt a longing for a kinship with my surroundings. I wanted out of the prison of books and institutions.

Some writers seemed to drag on endlessly. Their books and contributions were meaningful, but I often thought they could have been written better, more concisely. That was only my opinion.

I have read a great number of books in libraries, choosing from what I was allowed. Books can be wondrous things. Page after page, they let you search for your own answers, eagerly taking in the words with your eyes. They allow the mind to wander over what is written, decoding the pieces of consciousness streaming between the lines.

A book is a meeting of minds; two sentient beings, interacting across time and space, I was finding.

A way to time travel.

Some of the first ideas I remember exploring came from books on how things work, as well as from dictionaries and encyclopedias. I ached to know the names of the things around me, how they worked, and what they did.

I loved those compendiums of knowledge and delighted in finding a copy on a library shelf. I could get lost for hours studying the illustrations, tracing the working paths of mechanisms, and matching the numbered parts to the sidebars. I studied those systems intensely.

Often the librarians had to kick me out because I was curled up at a corner desk, eagerly tracing mechanisms until closing time.

In the early 90s, personal computing became a lot more prevalent. I started seeing these things being placed in libraries. They used modems to dial up an information server and access that server. This advent seriously opened whole new worlds for me. I felt comfortable in the digital space I was finding stored on these hard drives.

Once, I met a very odd character. I was about twelve or thirteen, skipping school and wandering through the libraries in my city. He was an oddly natured man with a head full of ideas that sounded crazy to me.

He kept insisting that the keys to life are in our names, not just in people's names in general, but in ours as Native Americans. He showed me some things in older volumes from the section of the library reserved for historical documents. The book he used was fresher, not very old, but it carried weight in the way he explained it.

I could not comprehend much of it, let alone what it meant. The language felt antiquated, not relevant to what was then

contemporary life.

***

As I'm sure she can attest, I found my mom's various textbooks early in life.

28

In her earlier years, I recall, she would attend various educational opportunities of her own. Her first textbooks I found were on electrical components and manuals on transistors and capacitors.

I found the concepts of storing and releasing energy are quite similar to feeding things through machines; the product goes in, and output comes out when you want it.

Hey! I've got a brain. Is it anything like that…? Not quite, I found out.

I have studied networking systems, electrical systems, computer systems, and even methods of cryptography, all for free. It truly is an amazing world we live in. People have built entire foundations of knowledge simply by making names for themselves, developing bodies of work, and finding ways to fit their contributions into the world.

***

Thereafter, I ached to set my own foundation of knowledge, to plant my own roots.

I took it then as my mandate to learn about the big, wide world I was naturally born into, and use any method of communication I had available to communicate my findings, or attempt to make my way.

29

I think I realized what that man in the library was speaking to me.

I started using methods freely, thanks to the ever-so-gracious Democratic Leaders who have fought for individual rights to be recognized, as well as expanded the utilization of technology for civilian life.

I currently send periodic reports over social media, always carefully disguising my messages so they cannot be decoded. They are simply observations, things I have seen, experienced, collected, or created to support myself as I walk among our people in this land we share. I pray you have seen them. I put them there for the world to see.

Their music is not quite like ours; it carries a different beat, just as I have always marched to. Still, I could always feel the soul of the person or artist speaking to me.

Whenever I was out, I listened to newer music hidden under my headphones, watching the world as I walked my path. Sometimes I even took pictures and worked them into framed pieces for someone to hang on a wall.

***

My ears were pumped full of Nirvana for most of my teenage years.

At around 15 years old, I met a girl in my neighborhood. A woman I later found, as she was four years older than I was. We started having unprotected sex, and eventually she became pregnant.

I had to be a man now.

I scoured the local area for employment in my skill area, "Anything I wanted to be." Yeah, no. It doesn't quite work like that.

I had no qualifications, and what the hell is a resume?

My first job was at Jim's Liquor. I was 16 years old. My job was a Courtesy; someone who helps customers with their purchases and cleans as directed.

At first, it was kind of cool. The store was near a big university campus, and I was invited to parties almost every weekend. But drinking and partying all weekend, the way those young adults did, never really appealed to me.

I loved helping people I was finding.

A lot of customers came in to buy their usual beer, while others browsed through the Microbrew or Wine sections. I especially loved walking into the Humidor just to breathe in the smell of the cigars.

The cigar guy, Eric, was always helpful in answering my questions, though he never let me buy anything for fear of losing his job. He would explain the different wrappers and ring sizes, and which types paired best with different liquors.

I never thought much of it. I just loved the smell of the tobacco leaves. Thanks to my mother leaving cigarettes out, and what I could convince older friends to buy for me, I was able to smoke, but never purchase.

Two guys I made friends with, who were roommates, played in a band. I recall their names were Jamie and Eliot. I'd attend practice sessions at their apartment. Even though it was literally one block away from me, it was kept in far better condition by their landlords. At any rate, they had this kind of punky-ska sound. Sometimes they'd let me sit in on drums.

I'd often express myself in punky-sounding ways and get in trouble with my bosses. I recall one supervisor at Jim's named Lewis. I said something to him once, and he replied, "If you say that again, I'll bop you on the nose."

Wow, fair enough, I recall thinking. Authority still exists in workplace situations.

Before this, we had gotten along great. We were both pool players, so we had played a few games while out, so I felt comfortable joking with him, as if I was one of the guys. After that, it seems as if he made it his mission to find every little thing to terminate my employment. I talked with the floor manager,

Matt, about it, and he said to just shrug it off, that he would have a talk with Lewis.

Later that week, I was in the cooler stocking the beer section. The cooler section at Jim's traverses the entire depth of the store. Eighty feet of cooler, each had a separate spot for various alcoholic offerings.

Since I was in the cooler, I had my portable CD player in my jacket and started playing some music as I was working. I hung my headphones around my neck and jammed away as I filled the empty slots.

I got about halfway through and noticed out of the corner of my eye someone standing in the entryway.

It was Lewis.

He had a look.

"We've been calling for you."

"Jim had me come push the cooler in preparation for the sale starting." Inside the cooler, we couldn't hear the intercom anyway. In fact, this was an issue I had brought up before, that there should be a speaker or light when we're needed.

He didn't say anything else, just turned and left.

Today was my Friday. I didn't want to take any of that toxic shit with me into the weekend, so I shrugged it off.

I finished my shift without further incident and clocked out. The next week, I was fired. No further explanation.

I had worked there, after school, riding my bike to and from, for ten months. I was devastated.

I solemnly nodded to the friends I had made in the cashier line and made my exit.

***

One night, after a long day of skateboarding, I was walking home feeling lost and dejected when I came across a new pizza place near Jim's called Papa Schnatter's. I walked in, got hired, and even walked out with a coupon for a free pizza.

That night, I hopped on a bus home, eagerly excited, carrying that pizza with a proud feeling. When I got home, I put the pizza on the coffee table, kissed my son in his mom's womb, and told her I had just gotten hired. I told her I'd be a manager.

She looked at me incredulously.

"I'm kidding. I just got hired as a pizza maker. But, it's a job."

She congratulated me on getting hired, and we enjoyed the rest of the evening.

There was a training/orientation class the next week, and I received my schedule and uniform. I reported to work on my first day early by half an hour.

I eagerly jumped in. Before long, I was slapping out the dough, driving the line. When I'd get far enough ahead, I would move down and keep pushing. We would easily keep up with the orders on the screen and have time to spare. In my downtime, I would clean up, nonchalantly joking with the other inside workers and whatever drivers seemed friendly.

By my second week, I had already been promoted to Shift Lead. "Wow, thank you," I exclaimed eagerly.

I attended all of the training over the next few months, eagerly devouring the training manuals. It was all fairly simple, in black and white, right in front of me.

On my days off from work, I would hop on my skateboard and cruise over to my friend Brandon's house a few blocks away. He had an older brother named Lance I thought was pretty cool. He drove a Chevy Nova, hiked up in the back, and had a pretty girlfriend.

I often envied them, coming home to Brandon's, which I considered a home away from home, with their doggie bags from whatever restaurant they had been at, while my stomach grumbled. I was always welcome to eat whatever I wanted there, but it never felt the same.

Brandon had another brother named Paul, who could be a real asshole sometimes. Once, Paul and a friend strung Brandon and me upside down in the basement and left us hanging there for what felt like forever.

We were only rescued when a mutual friend, Cameron, came over to see Brandon, or to grab a bite to eat after work, as he often did.

We yelled at the top of our lungs when we heard him open the refrigerator upstairs, his customary way of saying hi after he takes off his boots, so we knew it was him.

After what seemed like an hour, he sauntered downstairs, eyed both Brandon and me hanging from the ceiling rafters, "What did you do?" he asked with a shit-eating grin as he proceeded to take a huge bite of the sandwich he had made.

Brandon and I both said, "Nothing," as Cameron drew his knife from a belt holster and cut our feet loose.

Naturally, he let us fall on our own to finish the unwrapping. Gravity hurts.

To this day, I still feel as if Paul simply did that because I was friends with Brandon. But, water and the backs of ducks, I say.

***

I learned about physics, how physical objects act and react in space. It was unsettling, but soon I began to wonder if I was only a physical vessel carrying a mind, just a voice in my head.

36

Pssh. I slapped the thought away. That was not what my elders told me, nor any educator I had ever met. How could I believe such nonsense?

Doctors call this schizophrenia. I filed the thought away in my mind, my own Medicine Pouch, to draw from if I ever wished to ponder it again.

I learned about critical thinking skills; distinguishing fact from fiction, opinion from fact, due to my creative side as a person, I still try to create my own world from what I'm given; from what I can see and find.

***

One of the earliest books recognized in our nation's history is by a man named Adam Smith, titled *The Wealth of Nations*. At first, I thought it would be about the inherent wealth of our people. After all, wasn't our land stolen during the Trail of Tears?

I first encountered this idea in visual form, in a movie called *Avatar*. If you have not heard, movies are moving pictures. Stories are beamed onto walls or displayed on a television set using electricity, light, and sound. Quite the illusion.

At any rate, I was clearly wrong about the content of that book, so the observation I took away was simple: never judge a book by its cover.

Another story that stuck with me was by Mary Shelley, about a doctor who wanted to bring a creation to life. He cobbled together a human from dead bodies. It was a wondrous book, but I eventually learned it, too, was an illusion, something imagined and created.

Over time, I favored a number of what people call book series. My favorites, as I remember them now, were *Encyclopedia Brown*, *Sherlock Holmes*, and *The Hardy Boys Mysteries*. I enjoyed characters who discovered things as they went, because that kind of nature resonated with me.

I read about other monsters too, things that go bump in the night, as well as highly technical material. My mind eagerly devoured everything I could take in with my eyes.

I found myself drawn most to stories about character development. I was fascinated by how people grew, overcame trials, and solved the problems set before them. I especially loved Sir Arthur Conan Doyle and his creation, Sherlock Holmes.

Another figure I read about was Johnny Appleseed, who I later learned was based on a real person. In the story told to us in schools, he walked across America sowing apple seeds along his path.

What an odd thing to be known for, I remember thinking.

As for movies, I gravitated to documentary types mostly. Learning how past people dealt with life tragedies. I really enjoyed the autobiography Roots, by Alex Hailey; this led me to Malcolm X, as well as other vocal leaders for Civil Rights later.

Through living vicariously in the lives I read about, I was reminded of a thought I once placed in my Medicine Bag: am I a mind inside a physical vessel within a larger system? Systems are vast, filled with many moving parts. There is no way my individual mind could be part of that system… is there? Can my voice truly be raised?

A system can easily accomplish any monumental task, it seems, like building the Great Pyramids we see on our local television channels, or in our cities, our skylines from outside the city, what people call suburbs. To think about the sheer amount of ingenuity, dedication, as well as human blood, sweat, and tears, it took to build such monuments! Or, it could accomplish a small task, such as opening a door or elevating someone up flights of stairs. Thanks, Mr. Otis!

People do like to leave their mark.

All it takes is vision, strength, and courage to seek help, if need be, to get it done.

***

In my teenage years, I wasn't allowed to go to neighborhood schools. When I later asked my mom why, she said quite presciently that I probably never would have made it there. Makes sense.

I'm sure she detected my rebellious side more than anyone.

I longed to hear the beat of a drum, that resonating heartbeat pumping furiously with the songs of my people, heard for miles. Later, I would try to attend our Native community powwows, even though I often felt shunned.

The comfort of memories in a physical space is another observation I recorded here. Finding a sense of place, a home, comfort. Humans can walk the path of their birth and call the place where they rest their home. These sensations of comfort resonate in our hearts and our souls. They give us meaning.

My meaning, my sense of self-worth, what gave me a sense of place, I was realizing, was to be an ambassador of my people, for my people. To walk among everyone, share in their stories, walk in their shoes, and live the lives they lead.

Still, I was forever the brunt of the joke. The natural-born little guy who always seemed to be kicked while down, the salt from my tears stinging my wounds and staining my face.

Water off a duck's back, I told myself, and I shuffled off to entertain my next idea.

I learned about Miyamoto Musashi. His greatest teaching to me was to be flexible, like water. I also learned about Sun Tzu, a Chinese warrior who compiled his thoughts in a book called *The Art of War*. I eagerly devoured its pages.

The one vital takeaway I carried from it was that "war can be an illusion." That left me wondering, could life also be an illusion?

That clearly can't be the case; I am here. I see the things in front of me. I can touch them, taste them, smell them, enjoy their presence, and them me, I assume, since they are there in my presence as well.

Life is not an illusion. I confirmed that through the writings of Søren Kierkegaard.

René Descartes had clearly shown that things can be described in two-dimensional space, even by analogizing space as a ceiling. I learned about agrarian societies in far-off lands, entire alternative bases for economies. I studied Karl Marx and his critiques of capitalism.

Modern competing theories suggest that the universe is either expanding or contracting, that we may be living in a simulation, or that time travel may soon be possible.

What I learned through it all is that no matter what theories people hold, they can still band together to support themselves, just as our people have since the encroachment of white settlers on our land. It is in our very name, American Indian.

Nations have risen from the ground by the sheer will of the people who inhabit them. The intention to live is itself a physical manifestation of the will to survive, sustained by the inherited wealth of preceding generations.

It is grounded in us as a human race, the simple need to endure. Only we can ensure that the world's natural resources are cared for, so that those same resources may sustain future generations.

I looked to my role models, the people in my life. I watched the way they lived, getting up for work, figuring out lunch and dinner, taking care of themselves, putting on uniforms, and wearing masks to play their roles in the world. Some people even make a living from it. They call it cosplaying.

My grandfather will always be my number one role model. As a child, he told me to grow up and make a name for myself. I never knew what he meant until recently. But that man never wore a mask a day in his life. Only a smile, and a set of watchful, caring, tired eyes.

While I was growing up, my grandfather probably knew the battles that lay ahead for me, growing up American Indian in a land he had long understood was no longer his people's. I loved him dearly and will always miss the times we spent playing cribbage, talking, or watching his favorite shows. He would sit in his chair and laugh along, sometimes right on cue with the laugh track.

I always wondered why television is called "programming." Why not an agenda, schedule, or calendar of shows? They beam light shows of illusion straight into our eyes, letting our brains process the message. If we cannot see, we are given corrective eyewear or surgeries to make sure we can. They keep people tied to their televisions with stories of suspense, murder, intrigue, and capital crimes, all to keep them in front of the screen.

America truly is a remarkable land.

My grandfather was a boxer. He fought in the ring, dueling his opponents one-on-one. I remember him as humorous, hard-working, and generous. He would literally give you the shirt off his back if you were in need, or cash to help you on your way. When I arrived at his house, he always asked if I had eaten. I later learned this was a common way of greeting visitors among our people. We never knew if travelers had come from far away, so we greeted them by sharing our food and resources. We are a humble people.

I once read in a book that this practice had something to do with a ship called the Mayflower.

My favorite activity with my grandfather was playing pool with him. Over time, this connection of pool, memory, and space reminded me of my Medicine Bag. Into it I placed a thought: was I a physical vessel holding a voice in my head?

No. Once again, I am reminded of my experiences, my path thus far, and I certainly had more than a few scars by then.

One of my earliest role models is Bruce Lee. He was an American-born martial artist who acted in a few movies; I do enjoy his spirit! His philosophy in life was to pick up his own philosophy from things he encountered along his own path and develop those techniques into his own philosophy. He called this Jeet-kun-do. This definitely resonated with my spirit!

Some Western movies were okay. Chuck Norris and his Delta Force movies were also really great. I'd get lost in the fiction being displayed, although it was based on very real events and happenings. I especially liked the stories with strong character development as opposed to just the "shoot 'em up bang-bang" ones.

I am told we, as Native people, are special. Why, I wondered. So, I looked at our treaties. I looked at the intent of the relationship, to have good neighbors to help in a time of need. Wow! So that's why I'm special.

Looking back on my life, I can only see that my people, our people, the people I walk their paths with, the people that have invested in me to be the person I am, I can only see that my life has been institutional slavery since the moment it intersected with the State of Minnesota, when I was born. Driven by only the intent of past generations to drive forward, to the stars.

To acknowledge levels of humanity in us as individuals, free to find our own ways of seeing the world. I was reminded of that man I met in the library so many years ago.

***

I thought back to that chance encounter in the library so many years ago. By this time, I had developed the idea of redeeming myself. I had made a few bad choices in reacting to the abuse I had experienced thus far, and was on various forms of adult, corrective supervision throughout my teenage years. I would often discuss my future with my then probation officer, Ms. Steinwalz.

Overall, I believe she was a very fair person. She contacted someone on my behalf for an endorsement letter to enter into the U.S. Air Force ROTC program. I was maybe 17 at that time.

One day, I walked into her office to receive my weekly community service assignment, some job I could work off for my intrusion into adult life. She handed me a sealed envelope from a U.S. Senator. I opened the letter and eagerly read the contents. It was describing my recognition from him and an endorsement to join the U.S. Air Force, as well as a personal note.

His later death will forever remain a scar on my soul. He was one of the few people who truly recognized me as a person. The words in that note, and the intentions behind them, are emblazoned in my memory.

That Senator turned out to be the same man I had met in the library that day, back when I was skipping school. Evidently, I had made an impression on him simply by choosing the library over the classroom.

***

From then on, I continued the path I was on.

3

In my early adult life, I took a position as an Executive Assistant within my Tribal Government. I enjoyed being in this position, addressing the needs of the various people and entities that entered our department. A place where I can fit in, where I can reach out to people and get to know more about my world. A place to learn what I needed for my personal work. My life mandate.

My next role models were those I could fall back on and depend on: family, friends, and elders in my Tribal Organization. I learned about how fiercely we as Native American warriors are, in body, mind, and spirit. That we only wanted to live on the land we were given.

I quickly fit in, of course. Laughing and chatting with the ladies and gentlemen who entered or needed anything from our Department. I understood things like go, take, do, and put very well, and quickly worked my way into a permanent position earning more money per week than I felt I was truly entitled to, but they were paying me, so it felt good and rewarding.

In working there, I sought to entrench myself in the politics in private. In my training, I was trained in Parliamentary procedure and was never afraid to remind the assembled Commissioners if there was a deviation from procedure, or a motion still hanging.

I took my job very seriously.

In those days, there was a big push to unify our four districts and further establish reservation sovereignty; in contrast, local governments saw our presence there as an intrusion. Legal battles were fought in open court; boundary and gathering issue rights were frequently being challenged; law enforcement and constitutional officers tried to broker peace and extend helping hands wherever they could. It was an absolute headache for the Tribal Executives, I'm sure. I only heard snippets, but it never sounded fun to deal with. Interesting, but not fun.

In 2002, news reports everywhere were flying around that a Senator from Minnesota was killed in an airplane crash. I turned on the radio and was greeted within a few minutes with the news. Necessarily, I was heartbroken. I felt that an old friend had passed, even though I barely knew him.

***

But steeped in all of this material, I met Carol, my long-lost cousin, through a distant aunt named Jona. Carol had a boyfriend she loved, Lee. Their relationship was tumultuous. She once told me she had needed surgical intervention after he beat and kicked her during one of their intoxicated fights. Needless to say, I was stunned. But they were "in love," and I felt I had no right to interfere.

Granted, my own fights had always been against far larger people, but this was different. This was man versus woman, and as a man, I was appalled.

Before I allowed Lee into our home, a place of solitude I shared with my elderly grandfather, I told him plainly he had better be on his best behavior. He looked me square in the eye, promised he would, and we shook hands. The rest of that evening was filled with cocktails, laughter, and buffalo wings.

As stories were exchanged lightheartedly, I came to realize something strange: though Carol and Lee were like oil and vinegar, their feelings for each other were undeniably genuine, even if expressed in the most destructive of ways.

Later that night, while we were all attempting to get rest, I heard the sounds of a struggle in the room that Carol and her boyfriend had occupied. I could hear her in there yelling and screaming, "Get off of me! Stop! You're pulling my hair!"

Naturally, as they were in my home, I had to intervene.

I entered the room by kicking in the door and saw him on top of her, choking off her attempts to breathe. I ran in, pushed him off of her, and tried asking what was going on.

Out of the corner of my eye, I saw him get up. He attacked. We fought for a couple of moments, and I knocked him down again.

I tried then to mediate the situation, to find out what was going on. Carol started telling me he was trying to rape her. In the midst of her telling me, I saw him reach down and pick something up off the floor. It was a knife!

When he lunged at me, I was able to grab his arm and disarm him. When he attacked me again, I felt I had no choice but to stab him. I stabbed him once and only once.

Afterwards, I called the police, or they were called, I can't really recall. But I sat and waited to face the music. I made no attempt to run or hide, but I did give the investigators of my Tribal Reservation Police Department a trying 6-hour interrogation.

In the interrogation, I told them I left the knife in the room.

Come to find out, the entire State Bureau of Criminal Apprehension had searched everywhere, even the shallow waters of the lake our reservation bordered, for more than twelve hours. Yet one lone Native American detective found what their whole team couldn't, he reported discovering the knife in a bathroom drawer. I guess that's our skill as Native trackers shining through… or maybe something else.

***

In the ensuing aftermath, I was convicted at a jury trial and sent to the State Department of Confusion and State Correctional Institutions. I served ten and a half years in all, fighting for my freedom, educating myself, and doing everything I could to stay clean for the battles that lay ahead after release.

I prayed hard with the people and groups I felt comfortable with. Eventually, the brothers in our sweat circle recognized my abilities and granted me the honor of carrying the Pipe for our imprisoned Tribe.

In Native American circles, it is one of the greatest honors to be recognized as a Pipe Carrier. It means that those who trusted you believe in your ability to help guide them spiritually. For me, it was not something to be taken lightly. Carrying that Pipe meant responsibility, humility, and service.

While inside, I kept reading stories by Civil Rights leaders and people who always spoke up for what they thought was right. While in jail awaiting trial, I read the Bible three times. I had definitely seen it before. I had even gone to Neighborhood Church activities while growing up. One block in my neighborhood was in the Guinness Book of World Records for having the Most Churches on one city block; it was an advertised curiosity.

I was exposed to the writings of Huey P. Newton, Eldridge Cleaver, as well as any sort of fictional account I could check out, only up to five books at a time, though.

Somewhere in these volumes was my key to freedom.

While working as an ABE/GED tutor in the Education Department, and once even being recognized by the State Literacy

Council, I continued to pursue educational opportunities to broaden my horizons. I earned a Certificate in Paralegal Studies, completed some of the credits needed for post-secondary education on the outside, and achieved a Certificate in Writing for Print. Because of intervening legislation, I had to use my own money to accomplish these goals. It seemed the State didn't want felons to become educated, and every real opportunity for rehabilitation was being cut off.

I eventually found a company I could trust to take Power of Attorney over my financial matters and continued my sentence.

Along the way, I impacted many minds with my endless questions and offbeat responses. Once, a student across the room asked me for the answer to a problem. Without even thinking, I blurted out, "42."

After a few moments, he shouted, "How did you know?"

The truth is, I didn't. But when I walked over and looked at the problem, I was able to explain exactly how to get there.

***

I fought a few fights in prison, more than one type, too. Both physically and legally, as well as spiritually.

Along the way, I was losing my path.

While in segregation for several months due to a fight, and another fight that happened a day or two before I was to be let out from the first segregation sentence, I made major headway and found a legal theory I could use in my defense; a claim of a violation of Due Process in the 5th and 14th Amendment contexts; i.e. that my jury was mis-instructed on the concepts of self-defense in the home and were told a different legal standard; namely that I had a "duty to avoid peril" which meant that I had to retreat first, as Judge Russian from the County explained to my jury, before defending myself or another in my grandfather's home on the reservation. The theory had precedent to support it, and I began crafting. The State Supreme Court ruled in that case that the inclusion of the jury instruction was a violation and warranted a new trial.

I tried hiring an attorney to secure my release through the State's Post-Conviction Review process. From what I understood, she had a fairly decent-sized practice, but I would not personally recommend her. She seemed dense when I spoke with her, while I was conveying my claims and pointing out issues in the transcript. I had even hand-written a three-page letter, carefully penned with one of those tiny rubber segregation pens, not unlike the golf pencils you see at Mini Golf. I included citations to specific transcript passages I believed warranted her attention.

Ultimately, that turned out to be a bust. She didn't understand a damn thing and, to make matters worse, reeked of alcohol the one time she came to hear my case. I found her daft and deeply regret spending $10,000 to secure her services. Even the federal court later suggested she had perhaps been misinformed.

My later attempts to challenge her performance through the State Bar Association also proved fruitless. She was entitled to keep my money, even though she never did what I contracted her to do. The claims she wanted to raise sounded fine on the surface, but they didn't strike at the heart of my case, which was rooted in the Judge's prejudice and the improper jury instructions.

So, I filed my Petition for Post-Conviction Review without the assistance of an attorney. I was eventually awarded an Evidentiary Hearing. Judge Russian of the County recognized the legal claims I was raising. He acknowledged that there had been a de facto misstatement of law, one he himself had made in instructing the jury. But still, he required me to prove prejudice on his part in light of the facts at trial.

It seems logical to me that if you instruct people correctly on how to judge a matter, they will arrive at a fair judgment. Any deviation from that standard results in prejudice, especially in a hotly disputed case like mine. I was defending myself and a woman from an assailant in my own home. What duty to retreat could I possibly have? If someone attacks you where you live, in your own space of safety, what would you do?

In the end, my story was heard by twelve others. There were a few instances where the jury said they couldn't reach a verdict, but eventually they did, and I was condemned to sit.

***

In prison, there was an Appellate judge by the name of Judge Crandall who would visit and attend our annual feast and sweat lodge ceremony with us. He is/was retired, I cannot fully say. Once during our annual feast, in which he was in attendance, I was discussing in vague terms the legalities of my particular situation. I was picking his brain without him knowing it.

I asked him thoroughly about the intent of the due process clauses and how fair trials should be conducted. We exchanged a few questions and continued on our way. I, of course, thanked him very profusely for his knowledge in crafting my own arguments.

Jailhouse lawyers do exist. It's a shame that so many in legal situations truly do not get the legal benefits they are truly entitled to: active advocacy.

Later, when my post-conviction review and appeal came up, I learned my case had been assigned to this judge!

I anxiously awaited a response granting a new trial, with new counsel. Or an outright reversal as a matter of law and fact.

I lost on that claim. How can you prove a Judge's prejudice from misstating law….? Ultimately, my claims got shot down in all courts, including the federal circuit, and I continued to sit. By this time, I had neither the time left in my incarceration nor the ability to pursue the matter in the Highest Court of the Land.

More water off a duck's back.

I decided to take the knowledge I had gained from navigating my own claims in the courts and put it toward earning a Certificate in Paralegal Studies. What was meant to take a year, I completed in about eight months. Around that same time, I chose to continue my education further. By then, I had already earned a few credits toward an Associate's degree, along with a certificate in Writing for Print.

***

When I was released from prison, I felt dissociated again. I was not able to secure housing in any halfway house or program due to the severity of my conviction; nor was I welcome anywhere, it seemed. I couldn't locate housing in my County of Commitment, as State Law requires, so I had to seek out other arrangements.

The parole officers literally gave me about two hours to find and purchase a place or home, since I wasn't able to find an apartment or halfway house. I think I had about $6,000 in cash on me from what I was able to save from my meager wages inside.

Who the fuck can buy a house fresh out of prison with that? I wondered.

I tried all I could to secure housing. I purchased several local newspapers and a pack of cigarettes and got busy on the phone.

Between intermittent cigarette breaks and phone calls out, I pored through the classified sections. I called everyone, listing a place, including trailer parks, to find a rental.

I wasn't able to find housing.

Whenever I finished explaining my dire situation, the line would usually go silent, followed by a quick hang-up and the same response: "No felons."

The officer was nice enough to let me have a cigarette before I went back in for another 6 months.

***

A lot of the lifers in prison are actually quite respectable. Some of the older souls I identified with immediately.

I'd enjoy playing guitar, playing handball in the gym and on the yard, and I'd even enjoy the books in the library.

I was maybe three years in before I got ink on my arms. I went all out, at least in my opinion, and got two half-sleeves. The work cost me about $120 in commissary items altogether. Not bad considering the quality of the work.

In prison, guys fight all sorts of battles. Their pasts. The officers. Each other. But the hardest fights to watch are the ones that happen inside, the battles they fight with themselves.

I've walked past cells in Segregation holding men in what we called "Pickle suits," or sometimes stark naked in "dry cells" rooms without running water, designed to trap contraband smugglers.

I get the idea, but… Their house, their rules, I suppose.

I'd often see the Corrections Officers watching videos of fights; I turned my eye, but I knew what they were applauding and cheering secretly.

I just kept on my path. My path to freedom. Recognizing the chains I was in, and seeing how they could change.

***

Towards the latter half of my sentence, I guess my behavior and good conduct had warranted a transfer to lower custody level facilities. I enjoyed my time there actually. By that time, my legal battles were over, and I was just coasting until I got my go papers. I enjoyed my time on the handball courts and in the various courtyards.

In lower custody facilities, the program is a bit more open and thus feels freer. Prisoners are allowed to be out of their cells until 10:30 pm, whereas other facilities are locked down at 9:15 pm.

During my tenure at this facility, I kept on the path I was on. Helping to guide the other imprisoned souls that were around me. I helped guys develop business plans, develop projects, and give rightful advice.

One night, while lined up for count at our work assignment, I was horsing around playing with the Native brother who was in line next to me. One of the things we did was a "dead finger," where we would let a finger, often the middle one, go limp, then smack each other when not expected. I intended to give it to him as soon as the count was cleared and we were free to go back to work.

The officer saw me swinging my finger around down at my side. He reached for the mic on his shoulder and called for backup.

At the resulting hearing, I was being accused of flipping the officer conducting the count the bird.

I argued, of course, that it was false, that I was just loosening a finger that was hurt. And even if I had flipped the officer the bird, that kind of gesture is still protected under the First Amendment.

I lost.

The Department of Confusion Hearing Officer sentenced me to 60 days in segregation. While serving that stretch, I ended up in a section known as "In-House." That's where I got caught with contraband, weed to be exact.

My cellmate, a guy from Texas, and I were smoking and eating cookies, watching *Futurama*. That show hits different when you're high.

I timed it so we'd light up right after the Correctional Officers did their usual round. When the coast looked clear, we sparked up and blazed two or three fat joints, then sat back to zone out with the TV.

Not fifteen minutes later, a surprise round.

At first, the officer walked right past us. I thought, *Phew, we're good.* But then he stopped, stepped back, and I caught that faint smile on his face. We locked eyes. In an instant, his grin dropped into his "Mr. CO" face as he radioed for the water to be cut and called in an A-Team response, their code for backup.

Dammit, man.

He caught me, fair and square, as they say.

But I still made them search for the remainders.

I was put in a deeper part of segregation after that and told I would be awaiting more charges. Sure, bring it, I thought. I was on my way out the door, and would most likely get the time run concurrently. It did.

The sentence associated with that crime has been resolved, as have my other ones. I've pretty much just been finding my way again. Making art, telling stories.

Just an old spirit that forever wanders.

4

After being released from prison in 2013, just before Christmas, I was placed on the State's Intensive Supervised Release, hoops to jump through, since I had to have adults watch over me.

Fair enough, I had taken someone's life.

The day I was released, a guy by the name of Wilson Von Schmidt, a tall, bald, Nordic-looking bloke, picked me up. He explained that even though I was free, I still had to ride in cuffs until I was delivered where I was supposed to be.

During the car ride, he almost seemed genuinely interested in hearing my story. It was an hour to my aunt's home. But then, because of some of the terminology I was using, he got angry and gave me the evil eye in the rearview mirror.

"First of all, we don't use the term *caught…*" he started.

I mugged him back with the open-faced, blank stare I'd perfected over the years. *Sure thing, guvna,* I thought.

He was armed, and I was cuffed, so I didn't bother testing his authority.

Instead, I tuned out and let myself enjoy the car ride. When I tuned back in to his programmed spiel, he was saying something about taking me back to prison. I listened a little further and realized he was just going over their regulations.

I tuned out and enjoyed the scenery again, something I had been deprived of.

On the ISR program in that county, you have to file schedules weekly. There are times when you are allowed to stop and pick up store and hygiene items. But it is very much to the place, from the place, call on arrival at either. In addition, they can pop in on you, wherever you're supposed to be, as well as drug test or breathalyze you at any time. Also, this may have been a special rule in that county's jurisdiction, but you had to explain your case to any future romantic interests.

Once we arrived at the home of my family, he released me into their care.

After reuniting with my family for a bit, I settled into the downstairs bedroom they had set aside for me. I made a list of priorities. Clothing was first. All I had at that point were prison sweat suits and commissary-purchased tees, stamped with the Bob Barker name or the State Corrections industry label. I had to dump those fast.

They let me out on a two-hour pass to buy clothes. There was a mall nearby, so naturally, that was my first stop.

Being back in the world, I didn't know what I wanted to be again. In prison, I kept track of things in my head or on paper, building portfolios and accounts. I checked my finances. I had $5,400. When the Department of Confusion accepts prisoners back in, their exit money is taxed again at 10 percent upon re-entry.

The first thing I did was get licensed to drive.

I found a black 2003 Pontiac Grand Prix listed at a not-so-local lot, paid in cash, and drove away. Prior to this, my ISR agent explained that before I could purchase, own, or operate a vehicle, I needed their permission. This was to make sure I was legal with insurance and all. I understood, but I was very much my own person.

For about a week, I drove around after getting all the paperwork official and receiving my driver's license in the mail. I hid my activity from the parole agents, telling them my cousin was driving me or that I was getting rides elsewhere. Sometimes I parked away from the house, drove past to make sure no one was waiting for me, and if they were, I left the car behind the school next door and walked home.

One time, while on a two-hour pass, I was driving somewhere I wasn't supposed to be. The pass was scheduled for the local mall.

I was cruising through a tunnel when I got a call from one of the ISR agents. I ignored it and high-tailed it toward the mall. I didn't exactly break the speed limit by much, but I did cover the forty miles in about eight minutes.

I parked quickly and walked inside. My first stop was a big-name clothing store. I still needed a winter coat.

And there he was. One of the four ISR agents assigned to me, cruising the racks. I walked up casually. "Hi, looking for me?"

He actually looked startled.

"No, actually. I'm just here doing some of my own shopping," he replied.

"Oh, well, okay. Sorry to bug," I said, and walked off.

I went home afterward, called my arrival in, and sat down to homework. The next day, they called me into their office.

Damn, I thought.

I went and saw what they had to say, dreading, of course, the inevitable questions as to my whereabouts.

"Where were you yesterday. We called." No questions. Statements.

"I was at the mall. I wandered into Home Depot and must have lost service. Why?"

"When you're out, you're supposed to answer."

"So? I told you, I lost service. Out of my control. I did see him there," pointing at the ISR Agent sitting in the corner, not saying anything, knowing he'd seen me.

He looked stunned. "Yeah, I ran into him there," he said.

They said something I tuned out to and they made him file a report about having contact with me during his off hours.

After that, I registered my vehicle with them, though.

I enrolled at a local Community College after that, determined to at least finish the Associate of Arts degree I started, and I began looking for a job.

I secured a few interviews. I tested myself in the mirrors. I got myself confident.

Ultimately, any position I applied for would decline employment. I interviewed well and would often get secondary interviews. But when it came to the background checks, I was a felon. I received background checks declining employment from gas stations, grocery stores, supposedly felon-friendly organizations, everywhere I applied.

Finally, I applied at a temp service and got assigned a position somewhere. I wanted to fit in again somewhere, anywhere, even for the camaraderie.

I was offered a position as a Crane Operator at a local steel supplier. I was to be in control of handling upwards of 20 tons, over the heads and in the paths of people. I had to get training. Necessarily, I understood the physics very well, as a concept, as well as the safety concerns. They put me on what seemed to be the harder side, with another guy.

He was to show me the ropes until I could feel confident enough. I felt very confident, very quickly.

The second week I was there, the man who was supposed to be supervising me, since I still wasn't allowed to be left alone with steel in the air, left the area. I never knew if he went to socialize or just to use the restroom.

The production lines started piling up.

I grabbed the remote for the crane and began clearing those lines. Honking my horn. Making sure to observe all safety measures I had been directed to follow: maintain a triangle of height, honk the horn, and don't lift too much at once.

I was beeping the horn, making those bundles of steel I grabbed between the blades of my crane dance in the air. I learned how to compensate for the weight with the direction of travel to stop on a dime, or to use the momentum to turn the load manually, all while beeping my horn. I cleared the production lines and loaded trucks with ease.

The Big Man walked in. The man who signs the paychecks.

He knew that I wasn't authorized to be on my own quite yet. I kept about my job. Doing what he paid me to do.

"Where's your handler?"

I looked at him, open-faced, "I don't know. The lines were backing up. Try looking for him, and tell him I need him over here."

He looked at me, quizzically, shrugged, and sauntered off. I returned to my job.

The next work day started off with them calling me in the office, my handler, my supervisor above him, and the Big Man.

They explained that it was a test. To see what I would do. I passed with flying colors, and I was allowed to be on my own with that crane.

There was some employment paperwork pulled out, and we set about agreeing on a schedule. I explained that I was also attending college, and they would have to work with me on scheduling. That was all fine and satisfactory, and we signed an agreement for employment.

For four months, I worked there, making steel dance in the air, clearing the lines, keeping up with the machines.

On the side I was on were two machines for either hot-rolling steel or cold-rolling it and cutting to size in bundles, and both machines would break down constantly. Or one of the operators would frequently miscount his layers, causing me to fix his mistake.

This got to be very irritating. Every day, he would make some mistake or cause a backup on his line. I started wanting to go elsewhere if I heard his machine go down or stop.

Most often, I would have to pull top layers off to shim a middle layer for space for my crane blades to get in, and this was all a lot harder, as sometimes you had to be creative.

Other times, you have to get out special tools.

I would often see the guys using plasma cutters, oxy-acetylene torches, and a special tool called a Nibbler. I liked this name because it reminded me of Futurama. It worked by nibbling through plates of steel with tungsten-carbide teeth. It was a very interesting tool to use, and it was one of the first power tools I was allowed to use on my own there. Over time, I learned the basics of welding and cutting by watching the guys clearing the lines.

I would meet all sorts of truck drivers who came through to get loads. People from all over the place. One guy who came in would tip $100 if you could get him loaded up and back on the road very quickly.

I learned to recognize his truck and the orders he usually picked up. I studied their lengths on the pre-production sheets I had been shown the week before and figured out where they were in the warehouse bay. Easy, I noted.

I scrambled up on stacks of steel, standing thirty feet high, hopping around, horn blaring if need be. Clearing lines and loading trucks became routine. Before long, my handler left for another company, and I worked four months on my own, making that steel dance in the air.

One day, maybe from a bad mood, I snapped. The guy running the machine kept miscounting bundles. Every other stack was wrong. I tossed the remote his way. "Do it yourself."

He followed me out, shoving me, calling me names, trying to bait me into a fight. I reached my car.
"Look, man, fix your own mistakes. I don't have time for it."

He shoved me against the car and started throwing punches. I speared him to the ground and landed a few shots of my own. His lip split, bloodied. People began to circle. I realized what was happening and backed off. He got up and punched me again.

We went at it a second time until others tackled us. After a few minutes, we both agreed to cool down. They let me go, and I jumped in my car. Gravel spat into the air as I peeled out, rooster-tailing rocks and dirt behind me. I was done.

The next day, the call came.
"Where are you?"
"On my way to school."
"We have to talk. We can't have you assaulting our employees."
"Assaulting? I was attacked."
"That's not the story I'm hearing."

I shot back, "Did you not see me get followed outside?"

"I did, but he looks horrible today."

I barely had a scratch. He was taller, but grandpa taught me to close in on the tall ones. Take away their reach, and the fight is yours. "Not my problem," I said flatly, and jabbed the End Call button.

By then, I had two twelve-inch subs in the trunk. I cranked the volume on whatever was streaming through my Bluetooth and drove, thinking about my next move.

The following day, I changed my major to Art. The first elective I joined was Black & White Film Photography. All my life, I had collected mental snapshots of people, places, and things. I am terrible with names, but images stick.

My instructor was an older woman named Diane, an Italian-American photographer who, I later learned, had fought hard for the grant money that built the arts building. The place had a darkroom, studios, a computer lab, even hot and cold glass shops, all linked by a skyway to the main campus. On the tour, I was drooling. I could not wait to see what I could create.

We learned the basics: focal lengths, shutter speeds, ISO, how to focus a scene. Then we were cut loose to roam the grounds. I was hooked immediately.

I followed a trail behind the school into the woods, though it only led to a nearby neighborhood. Still, I walked back, clicking photos of everything. None of them were great, but to me, they were everything, a way to reconnect with a world I had been away from for so long. The development process would come next week.

Diane dismissed us, and I was off, running on my Chevro-legs to my next class.

***

It was around this time that I decided I'd like to socialize with females more. Females in my ASL class, as well as some of my other classes, were certainly very attractive. They were all much younger than I though. In truth, I felt old in those classes, but I looked younger than I was. I'd often get complimented on my cologne or my hair. The ladies have always loved my eyelashes.

I turned to online dating.

I chatted with a few women I met virtually while hanging out online. I had had a few dates, but nobody I found genuine. So, my disinterest may have been obvious. I hung up this idea again, placing it in my Medicine Bag, my memory. I'll try that again later.

At this time, I was sincerely interested in a younger woman who was a darkroom attendant and Student Resource in my photography class. Her name was Gloria, or the name she went by. I thought she was absolutely beautiful.

71

She had a pale complexion with darker hair. She would often arrive at school in gorgeous outfits, jeans and a T-shirt, or whatever she felt like throwing on, it seemed. But it all worked for me. She had a nice shape under her clothing that I found very appealing.

I slowly built up the confidence to start asking her photography-related questions. I would ask her how to do this or how to do that. Over time, it felt like we developed nicely as friends. But I wanted more.

I kept it to myself, though. I respected her. I chose to let it develop naturally if it did.

One day, I was walking out of ASL class with another classmate, and I saw Gloria at the tables in the Quad. I didn't think anything of it; to me, the walk I was making was platonic. We were going to study at the cafeteria and have a bite to eat.

She caught sight of me coming.

I saw her eyes flash from me to my accompaniment, then back to me.

Then away and back to her work, not even a glance as I passed, even though I said hi. I knew then that I had blown it.

After that, I respected Gloria's space and helped her celebrate her accomplishments in friendship.

Later that semester, she earned the honor of gracing the cover of
our school magazine with her photography, along with some of her
writing inside. I tried to make a big deal of it. I grabbed ten copies
and even had her autograph one for me.

***

I occupied a corner seat in my American Sign Language class.
My ASL Instructor was hearing and speech-impaired, so we
respected him. Plus, he could read lips very well. He signed as the
words flashed on the PowerPoint he was displaying for us.

This, of course, prompted a laugh, which he did indicate was
acceptable at that point. Text has a hard time conveying humor.

I had a great time learning a whole other method of
communication. My classmates and I would help each other along,
having full conversations in ASL.

I turned to internet dating again. I felt it was time. That's when I
met Maggie, and I was immediately drawn to her. She had red hair,
a pretty face, and when she "accidentally" called me one day, I
discovered she had a beautiful voice too. We chatted for a few
minutes, a little nervously, and set a date at a local art museum. I
even made sure to note it for the ISR submission later.

On the day of our date, I did my best to look presentable. I
figured she'd be just as nervous as I was, meeting someone from
online can be strange. I'd heard plenty of horror stories about
people getting abducted or assaulted, so I thought the museum was

perfect: public, but private enough to talk. We walked and chatted for about an hour before I had to head home and stay within my two-hour window. Afterward, I bought her a coffee, and we sat in the cafeteria, sharing more stories, laughter, and compliments. We promised to see each other again.

Not long after, while I was doing homework late one night and watching Saturday Night Live, I had this strange instinct to order two pizzas. Right after I did, Maggie called. She'd had an argument with her roommates, and they were threatening to kick her out. I invited her over, told her to relax, and offered pizza and some laughs to take her mind off it. She showed up within half an hour, and before long, we ended up in my bed.

I was a gentleman, though. Maggie was four years younger than me and very religious. She often brought up the Bible in our talks. I'd read it, but a lot of passages never sat right with me. Even when I studied apologetics and doctrine later, I always ended up stuck at the Council of Nicea. One night, I asked her if it was a problem that I wasn't exactly a believer. She looked me in the eyes and said no. I took her at her word.

I later found out she was enrolled at the same school. That felt like fate. We even signed up for a few classes together the next semester so we could help each other finish our degrees. Around that time, we were getting close to graduating together, so I doubled down and worked harder.

Eventually, I told her the truth about my past. I explained what had happened and why I went to prison, from my perspective. She was hesitant, but she didn't walk away. We agreed to meet with my parole agents so she could hear things directly. The meeting didn't go the way I hoped. The lead agent, the same one who picked me up from prison, seemed intent on sabotaging me. I had been honest with Maggie, but in that office, I was painted as far worse.

Water off a duck's back.

We left the interview several minutes later, allowed to continue our relationship.

Sometime later, I was allowed to graduate to normal parole supervision without further incident.

****

Along the way at College, I also studied: Drawing, Sculpture, Art History, Logic, a whole slew of brains to pick and learn from. I could literally stand on the shoulders of academic giants in these institutions. Given my particular personage, a member of a federally recognized Tribe, I was granted space to play and create. As well as learn more structure, chief among them is how to convey my wild thoughts from ideas to paper into an executable strategy. As my photography instructor said, "Artists secretly run the world." I could build whatever worlds I wanted in these digital and physical spaces. Only my own rules to guide me…my own creative license.

I took license with my creativity often. After school or class, I would go out in the area and practice my photography. By this time, I had upgraded from film to a pro-level DSLR, as well as a few nice quality lenses, and felt very comfortable operating it. I began exploring capturing more time in one frame.

I often felt like a time traveler, or an alien, absent-mindedly observing and processing my sensory observations, trying to figure out the space around me, and how I can fit in, or make the space in the frame reflect what I intend.

Much of my earlier work is just play. Stuff I noticed, felt compelled to share, and pass along. People began noticing my postings on social media and dropping likes and comments. That started to feel very rewarding. Naturally, I navigated to their profile and returned in kind.

On March 14, 2015, Maggie and I got married. By this time, Maggie and I had taken a basement apartment in her mom's recently acquired home. Due to my schedule, I would come home at inconvenient hours, causing undue stress on all of our relationships. In truth, Maggie, as well as her mom and step-dad, knew why I went to prison. Before we ever agreed to take her basement apartment, we had a family meeting where I laid out the details of why I went to prison.

Initially, it sounded amenable to all. Over time, and possibly somewhat due to the appearances I was giving, I started to no longer feel welcome.

Once, Maggie and I were playing hide and seek in the basement, and she let out a squeal of laughter. Immediately, I heard her mom come down the stairs, staring wild-eyed at us as we were in each other's arms, laughing and kissing.

She made some mention of bringing a shotgun the next time, and that I should be good. I looked at her, dumbfounded…

"Um, first of all, according to tenants' rights in this State, you cannot just come barging down here."

"I can if I want, it's my home," she replied.

"No. That is not the case. Landlords, even those renting space, cannot enter a dwelling without the tenant's permission. No matter the title of ownership."

She said something about being a smarty-pants. I shrugged off her retort.

"Look, Maggie and I were just playing. If there's some problem, say so."

She wagged her finger at me, "You just be good," and stomped back upstairs.

I realized, that this was perhaps a wrong step, taking the basement apartment, strategically speaking.

Up to this point, I had barely any free time to enjoy; my day was nearly 8 hours of class and studio time, as well as the little bit of design work I was picking up. Often, my day would have me arriving home after 10 pm, after I had started out at 8 am.

Maggie's mom had dogs. Dogs that would bark incessantly when I arrived home after 10 pm. This quickly became a nuisance to Maggie's mom, and I started getting weird attitudes and looks.

For a while, I shrugged this off as growing pains. The act of families growing together. I was respectful, but often, I really didn't have much choice; I had my education to finish, decisions I had made long before these instances, commitments to myself.

I started not going home. I would crash at another aunt's home. I didn't want to be subject to any authority at that point. I was on my own path before we met, and now I was feeling as if I wasn't welcome.

Of course, this move wasn't interpreted as the respect I was intending. The attitudes got worse.

Maggie's mom exploded at me. It felt a lot like that scene in Goodfellas, only I wasn't engaging in criminal behavior. I was being constructive with my time.

After this incident with her mom, I agreed to reconcile with Maggie if she would consider moving into an apartment. After a tense few weeks, she eventually agreed, and she located an apartment in her old building. The landlord was a fairly decent, older gentleman by the name of Che.

We settled into the apartment with some help and set up our living spaces and my workspace. Since we were both interested in photography, we agreed to do a studio in our living room and use the second bedroom as a sitting/TV room. After my years in prison, I could barely stand TV at this point. It's a distraction, or a pacifier. I would prefer to take my creative license out.

At this time, I had to make up one semester, that Physics class, and a few credits. I had met a few friends who were skateboarders, and I was working on a project I came to them with, as well as school. I was taking time off on weekends to pursue personal projects.

During the day, I was a student, at home I was a husband, on the weekends, I was at play. For me, it worked.

It was during the exercise of my creative license that Maggie would become upset. She had already graduated and started making money, and she often prodded me along, stressing about finances and comparing our situations. In truth, money wasn't really the issue. I'll admit, I was a bit sloppy with cash, which probably made it look worse than it was, but I had grant money in my account and the option to pick up temp work if I wanted. The truth was, I was still an adult student, fully immersed in school. My mind was on play, creation, and learning, but also on the future I was building. On top of that, my classes were spread out over nine hours a day. A traditional job wasn't realistic.

Maybe we should have had a deeper conversation about finances, about how I saw things and how she did. But in my view, I was the same person she first met, the person she was drawn to. I wasn't going to abandon that version of me just because I hadn't "arrived" yet in the way she wanted.

I often leaned into that creative freedom, sometimes leaving Maggie home in our apartment, or she would go out with her church friends. She was always safe. We had moved into a place in her hometown, the very same building she'd once been forced out of by her old roommates, which I realized later. But it was her choice.

We stayed there for a few months. I was still finishing up my last semester, making up credits for a failed physics class, while Maggie drove a school bus. Time together became a factor. My schedule kept me on campus most of the day, with short breaks that didn't make sense to spend commuting. We tried bridging the distance with social media, but that only went so far.

Over time, I started feeling like the goalposts had shifted. She wasn't just looking at me anymore; she was looking at a projection of me, a version she wanted to see in the future. But I was still me.

So where was I really going wrong?

***

I had set about learning how to use the computers and my cell phone to quickly dictate papers while I was driving or taking photos. In prison, I had my typewriter I would write on. The libraries had computers, but I left those for the guys who were doing their legal research and litigation.

I had to condense my time as much as I could. I was on a tear, and I really had no idea why. I had a wife now, and had to be a husband. I quickly aced most of my classes. I did poorly, actually, in Physics class. Which was kind of humorous considering my given history. But, it wasn't meant for me, I guess; some of the distance learning proved harder for me to compensate for. I later made up those credits in an Earth Sciences class that was more hands-on and to my liking.

Through my postings on social media, I was also gaining some recognition as an artist. I would use my skills to help draft contracts, as well as do some minor consulting. People who later asked me to help them. All I had to do was take some pictures of their performances, and I could enjoy a free show. For several months, I worked tirelessly building relationships with those

81

wanting to further their careers, capturing their performances in various nightclubs in and around Minneapolis, while also trying to maintain balance in my personal life. I felt myself teetering, but I was always a very driven person.

I saw my goals, and I was determined to achieve them.

***

Maggie and I ended up having an eruption. I was making dinner one night, broccoli cheddar soup. I'd spaced out and let it boil over. The apartment was still new to us, and in the moment of confusion I yanked the pot off the stove and hollered for Maggie to grab a spoon, she was standing right next to me.

Flustered, she couldn't recall where they were. The spoons were all in the dishwasher. By then, half the soup had already boiled over. Not wanting to fling hot soup around, I dumped the rest into the sink, maybe a little more aggressively than I needed to.

Maggie was indignant. "Why did you do that?!"

"Because there wasn't going to be enough for the two of us!"

She stormed out. I went out photographing. The apartment sat empty for two days. I stayed with family or friends, and sometimes in my car, gathering raw material for projects.

Not long after, Maggie threatened divorce. I didn't flinch. I filed papers. For weeks, she refused to sign, always with an excuse.

Finally, after months of delay, we met at my bank where she signed in front of a notary.

That night I posted the biggest smiley face I'd ever drawn on Snapchat. I was free again.

In 2017, I walked across that stage to claim my degree. Later I learned that less than 5% of Native Americans graduate from college or any other post-secondary program. For Native Americans with violent felonies, the number is closer to 0.3%.

I had conquered the biggest hurdle of all, myself.

I was free in ways I couldn't describe. I had stepped out of the hell of prison and back into my earth. But even then, a leash remained. The State still had me on parole.

By then, though, my supervision was light. Monthly check-ins, the occasional urine test. I told my Parole Agent I was an artist and photographer, that I liked the freedom to move around. She seemed genuinely interested, even impressed. I showed her some of my work, including one of my Instagram profiles. She recognized some of the locations and even joked about wanting to grab a beer there sometime, just not when I was around.

Not long after, I was released into "unsupervised" life. I expected that moment to feel monumental, but when the letter finally arrived, it was anticlimactic. Just another piece of paper with a State Official's signature.

I crumpled it up and tossed it in the bin.

****

Several years ago, I met my heart and soul. Her name is Hummingbird.

Meeting Hummingbird has truly been a blessing. Everywhere she goes, the room instantly lights up.

As I grew to know her more, I learned that her birth father had once marched with Rev. Dr. Martin Luther King Jr. She even had press clippings showing them together and everything. I was pretty impressed.

Later, when I got to meet him, and enjoy hearing the stories of these people that walked their fights to be recognized, I became more enthralled with redeeming myself again. I began plotting a new path.

Hummingbird was given up at birth by her birth parents. I never asked, they never told. It wasn't my business. But what was my business was the radiant warmth her curious, watchful eyes gave me. It felt truly rewarding to finally be recognized as a person in another, again. Not for anything other than who I was. This, to me, is my current blessing.

****

Our relationship started off as one of those love-at-first-sight moments. She was involved, as I was, with Maggie, so we kept our distance. But truthfully, I would secretly hope she would ask me to come be welcome at her home. Or even for a ride somewhere, as that would happen some days.

Our first encounter was at a bar in 2013. I was on the ISR Program still, and I was enabled to go on a 2-hour pass. When we met, she had the most beautiful smile and grace sitting there at the table. I honestly couldn't bear her beauty. I quickly made my escape to the patio area. I felt guilty, almost as if I had cheated on my wife or would, even though that was impossible. My sense of honor just wouldn't let me.

I occupied myself with my phone for a while, absent-mindedly scrolling through whatever social media was hot then. I think it was Facebook.

I heard a quiet voice: "May I have one?"

"Sure," I said, reaching for my pack. When I handed the cigarette over and looked up, it was Hummingbird. I fumbled a bit and dropped the cigarette I was handing her, right into the snow.

To date, we've been together for going on five years and I've never been happier. We still have little spats sometimes, but most often these are easily communicated with each other and we find a common ground again.

***

Fueled by my desire to create images and work in the skills I was trained in as an artist. I was out one night shortly before my fortieth birthday.

I had taken it upon myself to scout and scour for raw night skylines or city views in the city I was born in, or anything else that happened to catch my eye. At that point, the first COVID lockdown in the U.S. had been lifted, and I was tired of being cooped up in the apartment. Armed with three cameras, two digital and one film, my tripod, my cellphone, and headset, I looked around the city for interesting angles. Different light on different scenes. I scoured the whole city.

It seemed that during the lockdown, a lot of construction projects were starting up. I was seeing fresh scaffolding being erected, but not much of the beautiful lighting that my hometown is known for. The street lights were on, but no one was home, so to speak.

While crossing a street, after patiently waiting for the light to turn green, I was physically wounded by an officer of the City of Minneapolis Police Department, whether accidentally, negligently, or intentionally, I'll truly never know. I was in my own world, with my headphones on, crossing the street. But I am ever observant. Always conscious of my place in this world.

A marked police SUV came barreling around the corner, striking me.

I was rammed by the bars on the front, rolled by the force onto the hood, then unceremoniously dumped on the ground. That pesky gravity hurts.

Somehow, I have a vague recollection of being shaken, "Are you okay?" I viewed the scene from above my body, looking down.

There I lay, an Officer shaking me and one flagging traffic around the scene. When I came to, I heard her voice more clearly now.

"OWWWWW!!!!," I yelled.

I slowly rose to my feet and made my way to the side of the road. I was crossing a two-way street, and they were turning from a one-way. We both had green, but I was a pedestrian, and they were the authority. Their authority can kill, legally.

I sat for a moment, ignoring the questions. I pulled out my phone and texted Hummingbird: *"I just got hit by the police."*

I collected myself, still refusing to answer the officers. Behind me, I heard the driver pleading with her sergeant, "I didn't see him, I swear!"

I could believe that. People drive distracted all the time. I do it too. Pfff, I thought.

Somehow, I realized I still had my vape in my hand, but the top cap was missing. I scanned the scene until I spotted it, glittering on the pavement about twenty feet away. I staggered to my feet, clutching my ribs against the sharp pain, walked over, and grabbed the cap. I put it back in place, making sure the device was intact. Then I returned to the scene slowly, still holding my ribs.

By then, another officer asked for my ID. I handed it over. The next asked if I wanted an ambulance.

"Yeah, I think we'd better," I said.

Minutes later, the ambulance arrived. The medics looked like barbarians, wearing safety vests under their uniforms with tasers strapped to their hips. They went through their routine, checking me over. I told them where I hurt. They took pictures, had me sign a waiver of care at the scene, and left. I didn't feel safe going anywhere with them anyway.

I found a ride and was transported to the ER at another hospital. There I sat for hours in excruciating pain, poked and prodded with questions, scanned with machines, and injected with substances. I kind of liked the Dilaudid; it gave my mind rest, but I know how dangerous those substances can be to my Medicine Bag. I take them only with caution. I much prefer the sacred Marijuana.

***

I contacted a few lawyers about the case. The first firm I reached out to was a big-name operation with billboards plastered all over town. They were based in the same area where I got hit, so

I figured they'd understand my situation. They told me the lawyer who'd represent me would be Gus Meshbecker.

I looked him up, read some of his publications on personal injury cases, and even saw a few of his past settlements. *I can't go wrong here,* I thought.

Boy, was I wrong. I wouldn't recommend him to anyone. After that dead end, I kept searching but didn't have many options left.

Eventually, I found another firm willing to take the case. I've left it in their hands now. To be honest, I don't expect much.

***

My whole life to that point had come crashing to a halt.

Over the past few years, I've taken to vaping. For me, it's a substitute for the nicotine I crave. I still respect tobacco as sacred, but vaping became my outlet. At one point, I even started planning a device and managed to file a provisional patent with the United States Patent Office. I later learned those expire after a year unless you file for full protection, which costs a small fortune. I was running the numbers in my head, weighing what I could afford.

After my divorce from Maggie, my credit took some hits. A few hard inquiries, a home loan approval, and a lingering student loan problem left me with some damage. Quietly, I was working to rebuild my financial freedom. Chasing what they call the American Dream.

Through the physical pain of recovery, I've been forced to relive every beating, every dismissal, every moment of trying to explain myself to doctors and lawyers who couldn't seem to grasp the obvious. Since getting hit by that vehicle at around 30 mph, I've been through four ER visits, two rounds of diagnostic imaging, and countless injections and prescriptions that did little to help. They even handed me stretches off the internet disguised as "physical therapy."

I've never cared for opiates or narcotics, unless it's marijuana. Alcohol has never been my thing either.

Meanwhile, riots were spilling into the streets after a very public death. Protests spread across the globe, demanding democracy and equality in the eyes of the law. Conspiracies swirled. The world was seeking justice for a man who was a son, a brother, an uncle, and a father. His family and the families of many others would get their day in court.

But at the end of it all, I still wonder: who really holds the balance?

***

Our drive forward, for space, has led us all to a crossroads. Business transactions and the systems they've created now dominate our time, choking us off. What we need is simple: respect. Respect for the space we're given, the space we share. This one world doesn't belong to any one race, authority, or ideology. No one has control over me, my body, or how I choose to live in it, and no one should have control over you either.

The choices I make, how I act or react, are mine. Control is an illusion—or a delusion. They have badges, guns, tanks, satellites, even civilian drone strikes. And yet we're told this is for our safety. But is it really? Safety creates control, and control creates safety. My question is: who actually controls either?

I may be angry, hurt, sad, or frustrated. But does that give me the right to intrude on another's space? Unless I'm truly standing for something greater, the answer is no. My money doesn't entitle me to yours, and what little I have doesn't give me the right to flex over anyone else. This world was built by hands washing each other, engineers employing artists, artists shaping homes, designing cities, even imagining new worlds.

I've come to realize the future doesn't just lie "out there." It lies in each of us, and in the present work we do to live in harmony and carve out our space among the stars. Our future as a people of this world depends on the memories we share, the stories we pass forward, and the inspiration we leave behind.

The only thing truly concrete in this world is our impact on it.

All my life, I've tried to work inside the system, finding my way. I'm a Native American, born into a land that wasn't mine long before my birth. Yes, I've made mistakes, who hasn't? But I keep moving, keep building, keep writing.

Maybe that's all we really have: our voice. This is mine. If these words touch you in any way, know that my only intention is to make things right, as I see them.

***

During my imprisonment on this Earth, as we stand on the edge of a new Space Age, I believe Indigenous People, wherever they may be, should be recognized. Everyone, everywhere, deserves the right to exist and develop freely. No one has the right to interfere with another's path. Growth must come naturally, with accountability for our actions and the lessons we take from them.

A system itself is one big, self-contained sphere. A floating ball in space. A spinning mass of physical matter, moved by unseen spiritual forces.

[Sidebar:]
Have we been abandoned by our Creator? Or placed here with intention?
I don't know. What I do know is that I was born here, same as you.

***

No single person, entity, or group has dominion over you. Maybe there are aliens. Maybe there are rights we haven't yet discovered that will matter to us all in the future. The truth is, no one really knows.

The future is unforeseeable.

I write this letter having lived the life I've lived, knowing that we, as people, are enslaved only to our time here, until we buy our ticket elsewhere. But while we're here, we have to ground ourselves in common principles. We have to keep lifting each other up. People reach for the stars, as they say. I may as well reach too.

I've always walked in the moccasins I was given, one foot in the past, the other in the future. Today, everyone is told to mask up. Get vaccinated. Stay apart. As for me, I'll self-isolate, heal from my injuries and my deeper pain, and write.

All I have now are these memories: of growing up Native American, and once believing in the American Dream. I will leave you with the words from that note; words that have helped me define my dream:

"NEVER LET THEM LOCK YOU UP"